Bunny Day!

Adapted by Jenne Simon

from the teleplay by John May and Suzanne Bolch

SCHOLASTIC INC.

Published by Scholastic Inc., *Publishers since 1920.* SCHOLASTIC and associated logos are trademarks
and/or registered trademarks of Scholastic Inc.

The publisher does not have any control over and does not assume any responsibility for author or
third-party websites or their content.

This book is a work of fiction. Names, characters, places, and incidents are either the product of the
author's imagination or are used fictitiously, and any resemblance to actual persons, living or dead,
business establishments, events, or locales is entirely coincidental.

ISBN 978-1-338-11279-5

10 9 8 7 6 5 4 3 2   17 18 19 20 21

Printed in the U.S.A.   40
First printing 2017
Book design by Erin McMahon

It was almost Sparkle Bunny Day, and everyone in Charmville was egg-cited, especially Hazel!

She was only a Little Charmer, but she hoped her mother would let her help magic the eggs for the Sparkle Bunny to hide.

"Please-please-please!" she begged.

Hazel was full of sparktastic ideas to make each egg sweet . . . and special. Eventually her mother agreed that she could help.

"Remember, Hazel, the whole town is counting on you," she said.

"You won't be sorry, Mom!" Hazel called as she gathered the eggs and headed for the Charmhouse.

When she arrived, she found her best friends Lavender and Posie already there. They had jobs for Sparkle Bunny Day, too.

"It's too bad you're going to be so busy," Posie told Hazel. "We could have had so much fun doing our jobs together!"

"Maybe I could help you," suggested Hazel. "Just for a little while?"

"We could help each other!" said Lavender.

Hazel smiled. "'Cause one is fun . . . !"

"But three is charm-y!" they all cheered.

Posie was in charge of helping the Dancing Daffodils rehearse their dance—and they needed a lot of practice!

Lavender had signed up to decorate Sparkle Bunny baskets for the whole town.

The Little Charmers were having a totally charming time. But they had more work to do!

Hazel still had to magic the eggs for the Sparkle Bunny. Each egg had to be unique with its very own charm. That's what made them so sparkle-special!

The three Charmers worked together, singing a song as they worked. Hazel made a chocolate bunny egg. Posie made an egg with a golden locket. They even made an egg with giant feet!

But there were so many eggs to magic! It was getting late, and Hazel was starting to think they would never finish. She needed a magical shortcut . . .

"Sparkle up, Charmers!" she said as she raised her wand to cast a spell:

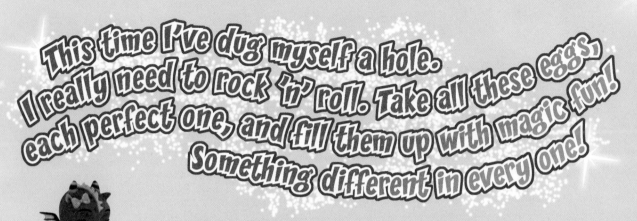

This time I've dug myself a hole. I really need to rock 'n' roll. Take all these eggs, each perfect one, and fill them up with magic fun! Something different in every one!

With a flash of magic, the eggs were transformed—and not a moment too soon! The Little Charmers had to get to bed. They had a very big day tomorrow.

The next morning, Hazel woke up and looked out the window toward the Charmhouse. The Sparkle Bunny had arrived . . . but he didn't look happy. "Chocolate chickens!" she heard him cry.

Hazel had to find out what was going on!

When she got to the Charmhouse, the Sparkle Bunny was pacing in front of the door.

"No polka-dotted eggs. No striped eggs. No eggs with funny faces," he said. "No eggs at all!"

Hazel couldn't believe it. The eggs were not on the Charmhouse floor where she'd left them. They were gone!

Hazel called her friends for help. "Magic can be messy," she told them. "But does this mess look normal to you? What if the eggs were . . . stolen?!?"

"Who would steal the Sparkle Bunny's eggs?" asked Lavender.

They decided to look around the Charmhouse for clues.

The Sparkle Bunny found a puddle filled with algae. Lavender spotted cookie crumbs on the windowsill. And Posie found a pillow stamped with a big muddy footprint.

Hazel thought they should start with the first clue.

"To the frog pond!" she declared.

But the eggs weren't there. Ferg the Frog Prince told Hazel that he and the other frogs had been making their Sparkle Bunny Day hats all night. It was a frog tradition!

"Then how did pond water get into the Charmhouse?" Lavender wondered aloud. "Oh! I forgot! Yesterday morning Ferg helped me with an egg-speriment! The pond water must have been from that."

The crumbs clue led the Little Charmers to Gingerbread Alley.

But the Gingerbread Boy hadn't been to the Charmhouse, either.

He'd spent the whole night looking for his gingerbread dog, Snaps.

Hmmm, thought Hazel. *I guess we'll have to keep looking.*

Next they headed to Ogre Valley. There they found an ogre who admitted he went to the Charmhouse last night. He had wanted to see the eggs so he'd know what to look for during the egg hunt.

"But I didn't even get a good look at them—they were moving too fast, rocking and rolling all over the place!"

"Rocking and rolling. Why does that sound familiar?" wondered Hazel. She thought and thought, and then remembered the words of the spell she'd used to magic the eggs. "Snapdragons! I know what happened!"

She grabbed her friends and headed back to Gingerbread Alley.

"I don't get it," said Posie. "What are we doing here?"

"Let's ask Snaps," said Hazel. "C'mere, boy. Bring us the ball!"

Only the ball wasn't a ball at all. It was a rocking and rolling magic egg! Hazel explained that while Snaps was out playing last night, he must have seen the open door to the Charmhouse—left that way by the ogre—and gone in to investigate.

"He saw those rockin' and rollin' eggs and couldn't help himself!"

"Snaps does love to chase things," said the Gingerbread Boy.

"But where are the eggs?" asked Lavender.

The Gingerbread Boy blushed. "He also loves to bury things."

"Mystery solved," said Hazel. And now she had a plan that would make sure the whole town had fun at the egg hunt.

Later that morning, everyone in town gathered for the Sparkle Bunny Day celebration. But this year, instead of searching for hidden eggs, they dug for buried ones in front of the fountain—Snaps's favorite burying spot!

The Sparkle Bunny Day egg hunt was a huge success!

"Thanks for not being mad at me for messing up the eggs," Hazel told the Sparkle Bunny.

"Are you kidding?" he said. "I got to see frogs and ogres and walking, talking, barking gingerbread. This was the best Me Day ever!"

The Little Charmers watched the Sparkle Bunny hop away.

"See you next year?" called Lavender.

"We promise not to lose your eggs," added Posie.

Hazel just laughed. "Happy Sparkle Bunny Day, everybody!"